To Frankie and Finn, sweet as milk and honey

— M. Sadler

To Simone, Teale, Nolan

— M. Slack

Text copyright © 2012 by Marilyn Sadler
Illustrations copyright © 2012 by Michael Slack
All rights reserved / CIP data is available.
Published in the United States 2012 by
Blue Apple Books, 515 Valley Street, Maplewood, NJ 07040
www.blueapplebooks.com
09/12 Printed in Dongguan, China
ISBN: 978-1-60905-188-4

2 4 6 8 10 9 7 5 3

MARILYN SADLER

PASS IT ON!

Illustrations by
MICHAEL SLACK

BLUE APPLE

One day Bee went to visit his friend, Cow.

Bee looked in the barn.

He searched down by the river.

He even checked under the apple tree.

Finally, Bee found Cow in the back field.
Cow was stuck in the fence!
Bee offered to find help.

I will
get help!

Bee buzz-buzzed to Frog's pad
and said:

Cow is stuck
in the fence.
PASS IT ON!

Frog quickly hop-hopped to tell Pig.

Frog said:

Cow put a duck
in the tent.
PASS IT ON!

Pig trot-trotted to tell Goose.

Pig said:

Cow's tent fell on a woodchuck. **PASS IT ON!**

Goose waddle-waddled
to tell Dog.

Cow and Hen
had good luck!
PASS IT ON!
said Goose.

Dog ran to the house and barked at Kitten.

A good duck
gave Cow a penny.
PASS IT ON!

said Dog.

Kitten ran inside and
meowed to Mouse.

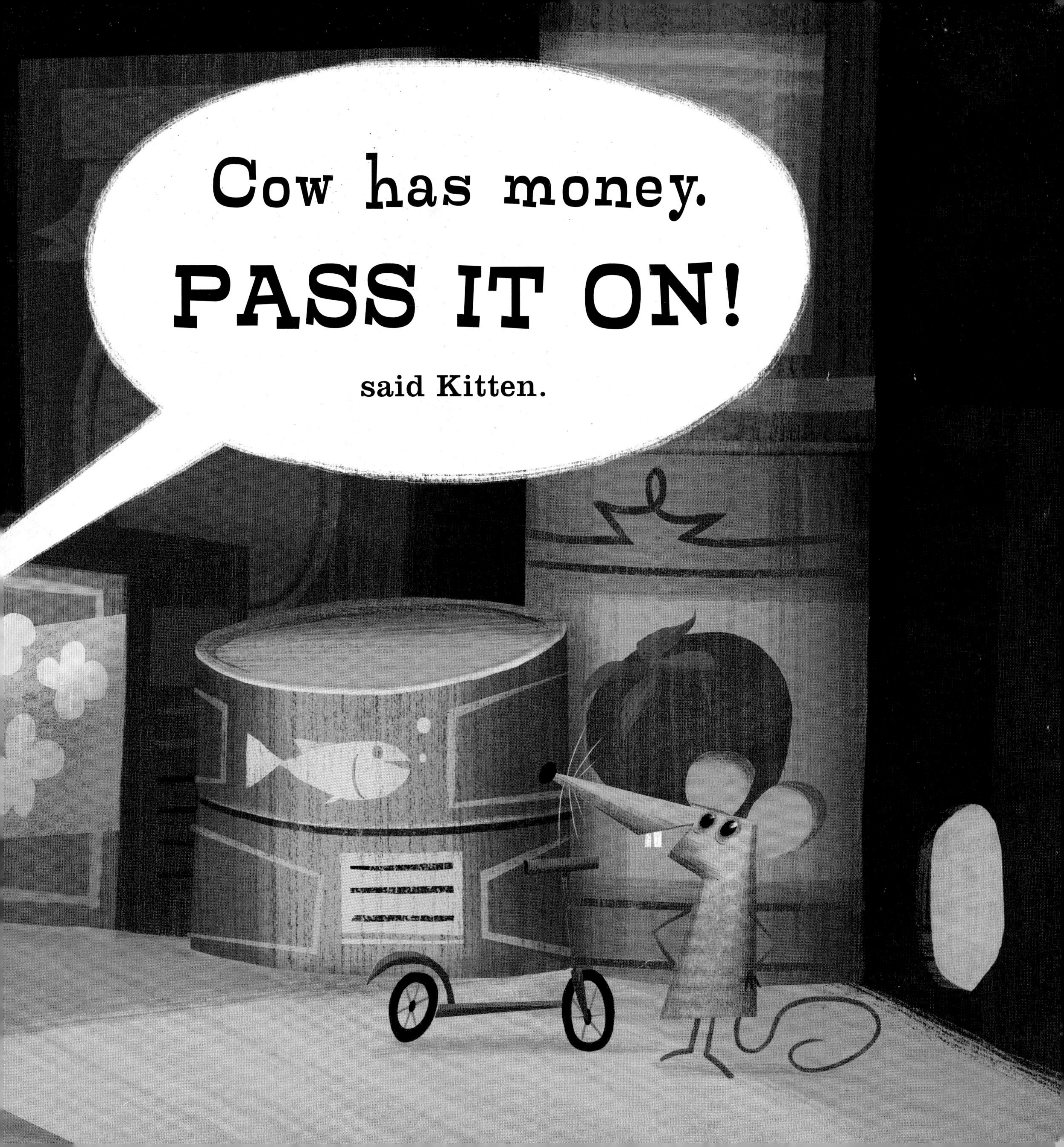
Cow has money.
PASS IT ON!
said Kitten.

Mouse rushed outside and
down the hill to tell Hen.

Cow has milk
and honey.
PASS IT ON!
said Mouse.

"Mmmmm," said Hen.
"I like milk and honey.
Now I'm hungry."

Hen and Mouse went to find Cow to get some milk and honey. What they heard was . . .

Then Cow invited everyone
who helped
to the barn for milk.

And Bee passed the honey.

PASS IT ON!